GRANDPA

by Barbara Borack

pictures by Ben Shecter

Harper & Row, Publishers   *New York, Evanston, and London*

for my mother and father

My cousin has to call him Uncle Jack.
But I can call him Grandpa.

In the morning I can see
Grandpa's socks and Grandpa's pajamas and Grandpa's robe.
But no Grandpa. He is hiding on me.

I always find him though
because he hides in the same place every time.
BOO!

Then we both get washed.

My grandfather always nicks himself shaving.
He walks around with a piece of wet tissue
on the cut until it heals.

When we went to the beach once

I covered my legs with sand

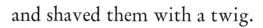
and shaved them with a twig.

He likes soft-boiled eggs best.
Second best is soup.
He goes *sssp, sssp*.
I go *sssp, sssp* too.
Grandma says we make a pair.

One time before anyone else was awake
we went for a walk to the park.
We had a bag full of oranges.
They were sweet and sticky and after we finished
the sun came up.

Then we licked our fingers.

Grandpa lets me help him at the store.
I stand behind the counter and write numbers on a pad.
When Grandpa is busy with a customer,
I draw pictures.

The back room is dark and
full of dusty boxes, silver key chains, and colored spoons.
I can have whatever I want.
Grandpa said.

Sometimes he lets me wear one of his shirts.
We stand in front of Grandma and she says,
"Just like twins.
Which one is Grandpa and which one is Marilyn?"
We tell her to guess
and she always guesses wrong.

Behind the door is a big glass jug.
Grandpa puts pennies in it.
plink, plink, plunk
He gives me some to put in too.
plink, plink

No one else knows about it.
plunk

He comes over to me and snips off my nose
and holds it between his fingers.

I say, "Grandpa! Grandpa!
Please give me back my nose!"

I sit on his leg and hold on to his hands and we play horse.

giddiyup,
giddiyup,
faster
FASTER!
whoa, horse, *whoa*

Sometimes he tickles me.
I say, "Stop! Stop!" and he always does.

My grandfather can make noises like chickens.
All my friends laugh.

And he makes hats out of paper especially for me.

I hate when company comes.
So does Grandpa.
So we both sit quietly
in the corner where the candy is
and eat it up.

When I knocked over Grandma's best vase,
everybody yelled at me.

But Grandpa said,
"Come, honeybunch, let me put a Band-Aid on your finger."

I like Band-Aids,
so he put them on all the fingers.

Grandpa sits by the radio and listens and stares.
I listen too.
We don't say anything to each other
and it's all right.

Once I wrote a letter to him
when he was sick in the hospital.
It said:

Dear Gramps,
    How are you? Fine, I hope.
        Love and XXXXX,
        your granddaughter, Marilyn

And I drew a face.

He wrote me a letter back
but it's private.

When I go away
Grandpa and Grandma give me a sandwich kiss.
Sometimes I am a tunafish sandwich.
Sometimes a banana sandwich.

They say, "What are you today?"
I say, "A pickle sandwich!"

My grandfather is old.
Here is a song I made up:

Grandpa Grandpa
I love you
and so do all the chickens.
Grass is green
and the pennies are brown.
It takes the sun
a long time to go down.
Grandpa Grandpa I love you
Yes I do.

He wears soft shirts and tan sandals with socks.
Nothing scratches me when I hug him.